The Rugrats' Book of Chanukah

Based on the TV series *Rugrats* created by Klasky/Csupo Inc. and Paul Germain as seen on Nickelodeon

SIMON SPOTLIGHT
An imprint of Simon & Schuster
Children's Publishing Division
1230 Avenue of the Americas
New York, New York 10020

Manufactured in the United States of America

10 9 8 7 6 5 4

Library of Congress Catalog Card Number: 97-65546

ISBN: 0-689-81676-6

#37821881

The Rugrats' Book of Chanukah

RUGRATS™

Adapted by Sarah Willson

Illustrations by Barry Goldberg

Simon Spotlight/Nickelodeon

Phil tossed a dreidel to Lil, who immediately put the toy in her mouth. Tommy chased Chuckie with a wrapping-paper tube. The babies were listening to Grandma Minka read the story of Chanukah.

"Hush, *kinderlach*," Minka scolded gently. "Don't wake Grandpa Boris. He likes to sleep when he hears a good story."

Didi was in the kitchen making latkes. As the lovely smell of potato pancakes wafted under his nose, Grandpa Boris woke up. Minka closed the Chanukah book, and she and Boris went to help Didi in the kitchen.

"What *is* Chanukah, anyway?" asked Chuckie.

"I don't know," said Tommy, "but every night I wear a funny hat and Mom lights another candle. Then I get a present."

Angelica rolled her eyes. "Chanukah is that special time of year when all the bestest holiday shows are on TV. Now quiet! It's almost time for the Cynthia Christmas Show!"

Suddenly Grandpa Boris let out an angry howl from the kitchen. He waved the newspaper at Minka and Didi. "Shlomo's picture is here instead of mine!" he spluttered. "Why does he get to be the big fancy-schmancy star? What will he do next? This will be the end of me!"

"Now, now, Dad," said Didi as she wrapped up the latkes. "He's not as bad as all that. Come on, kids. It's time to go to the synagogue. Grandpa Boris is in a play about the meaning of Chanukah!"

Tommy looked worried. "The Meany of Chanukah is going to get Grandpa Boris! What should we do?"

"Hmm," said Chuckie thoughtfully. "Once when a meany was mean to me, the teacher came over and made us both take a nap."

"That's it, then," said Tommy. "We'll find the Meany of Chanukah and make him take a nap! Then maybe he'll stop being mean to Grandpa Boris."

Meanwhile, Stu was busy working on a huge menorah down in the basement. "Go on ahead, Didi!" he called. "Pop and I will take my car. I'm going to fix this menorah so it's better than ever!"

"All right, Stu, but don't be late!" said Didi. "The rabbi is counting on you to light that menorah at the end of the play!" Didi, Boris, and Minka loaded the babies into the car and set off for the synagogue.

"Don't worry, Angelica," said Didi as the car pulled up to the synagogue.
"We're taping the Cynthia special so you won't miss anything."

As soon as the grown-ups' backs were turned, the babies went to look for the
Meany. Angelica decided not to take any chances. She went off to find a television.

The grown-ups took their seats in the audience. "I wonder what's keeping Stu?" said Didi worriedly. "He has to be here to light that menorah."

Stu and Grandpa Lou were stuck in a Christmas parade. "I told you not to take a left on Elm," growled Lou.

The play was about to begin. Grandma Minka was absorbed in her knitting and didn't notice the babies moving closer to the stage. The curtain opened.

"It's Grandpa Boris!" cried Tommy. The babies watched in horror as another actor came onstage and began poking Grandpa Boris with his fake sword.

"It's the Meany of Chanukah!" gasped Tommy. "Let's go!" The babies charged.

A few minutes later the babies found themselves in the synagogue nursery. Angelica was there, too, looking grouchy.

"What happened to you guys?" she asked, looking at their snuffling faces.

"We tried to save Grandpa Boris from the Meany of Chanukah," said Chuckie. "We were going to put the Meany down for a nap so he'd stop being mean to Grandpa Boris."

"But then the grown-ups put us in here," Tommy said sadly.

Angelica was thinking. Then she smiled. "You're going about it all wrong," she said slyly. "Don't you remember how Grandpa Lou falls asleep the second he sits in front of a TV? TV is like a lullaby for grown-ups. And I know where we can find one!"

Angelica led the babies down a hallway. "There's one," she said, pointing to a TV. "Come on! Give me a boost!"

The babies crowded together. She climbed on top of them and grabbed the TV. Then she cackled with glee. "Now I can watch my Cynthia special!" she shouted triumphantly.

"But wait!" cried Tommy, following her down the hall toward the stage door. "What about the Meany? I thought we were going to use this TV to put him to sleep!"

"Ha! You dumb babies!" said Angelica. "There is no Meany of . . . OOOF!" She had run right into someone's legs. The TV landed with a crash. The babies looked in horror. It was the Meany!

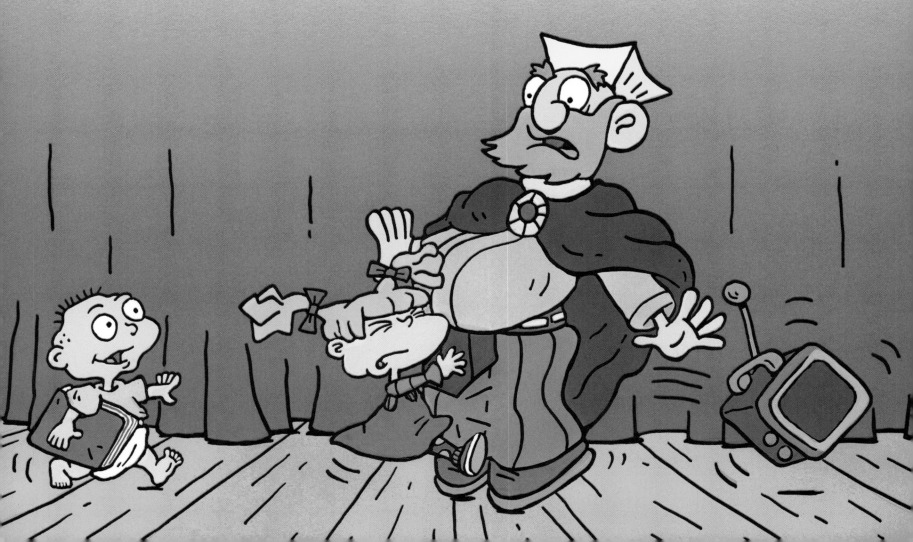

Angelica wailed. The Meany looked confused.

"What's he gonna do to her, Tommy?" whimpered Chuckie.

Tommy had an idea. He picked up his Chanukah book. "Remember how Grandpa Boris takes a nap when he hears a good story? Maybe the Meany will, too!" Holding the book, he bravely toddled over to the Meany. The others followed from a cautious distance.

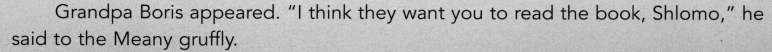

Grandpa Boris appeared. "I think they want you to read the book, Shlomo," he said to the Meany gruffly.

"B-b-but I don't know anything about babies!" said Shlomo. "I never had any myself!"

"Just read," said Grandpa Boris.

So Shlomo read to them the story of Chanukah. When he got to the part about the menorah, he stood up to light a candle. "A menorah," he said, "is like a night-light for our people." The old men and the babies were bathed in the glow of the menorah.

"And to this day," continued the Meany, "we light the menorah to remember the miracle of Chanukah." He smiled at the babies. Then he smiled at Grandpa Boris.

At that moment, Stu and Grandpa Lou arrived carrying the gigantic menorah.
The rabbi hustled Stu onstage. Stu threw the ON switch.

Pop! Splatch! The menorah lit up like fireworks. Then the lights in the synagogue went out and the curtain rose.

There were Grandpa Boris and the Meany standing together on the stage. "Look, Didi!" gasped Grandma Minka. "They're friends!"

The Meany of Chanukah stood up and turned to the audience. "My dearest Chanukah wish is that our *kinderlach* continue to carry the light of our people for generations to come." He and Grandpa Boris linked arms and began to dance.

"Look, Tommy," said Chuckie. "It worked. The Meany and your grandpa are playing nice!"

Tommy smiled. "It's a *mirable*!" he said.

THE STORY OF CHANUKAH

Long ago in the land of Israel, the Jewish people lived happily with their Greek neighbors.

But one day King Antiochus rode into town. He wanted everyone to be just like him—to read the same books, wear the same clothes, and even worship the same gods. Most Jewish people did not like this new way of life.

Judas Maccabee, a brave leader, stepped forward to challenge the king. He led his people to battle against the evil king.

The king was driven away, but the cities and temples were destroyed. The Jewish people repaired their temples. However, their beautiful menorah, which was supposed to burn forever, had been put out, and the Greeks had taken most of the oil. There was only enough left to burn for one night.

They lit the menorah anyway. Eight days passed and it still burned. It was a miracle!

To this day, we light the menorah every year to remember the miracle of Chanukah.